JAN -- 2023

To children—
May they keep
their creative hearts
forever

Every child is an artist. The problem is how to remain
an artist once one grows up.
—Pablo Picasso

Copyright © 2022 by Schiffer Publishing, Ltd.

Originally published as *Enciclopedia dei miei amici immaginari* by Bimba Landmann
www.bimbalandmann.com
© 2021 Camelozampa, Italy

Translated from Italian by Margaret Greenan

Library of Congress Control Number: 2022932094

All rights reserved. No part of this work may be reproduced or used in any form or by any means—graphic, electronic, or mechanical, including photocopying or information storage and retrieval systems—without written permission from the publisher.

The scanning, uploading, and distribution of this book or any part thereof via the Internet or any other means without the permission of the publisher is illegal and punishable by law. Please purchase only authorized editions and do not participate in or encourage the electronic piracy of copyrighted materials.

"Schiffer Kids" logo is a registered trademark of Schiffer Publishing, Ltd.
Amelia logo is a trademark of Schiffer Publishing, Ltd.

Type set in Sofia/Acari Sans

ISBN: 978-0-7643-6485-3
Printed in India

Published by Schiffer Kids
An imprint of Schiffer Publishing, Ltd.
4880 Lower Valley Road
Atglen, PA 19310
Phone: (610) 593-1777; Fax: (610) 593-2002
Email: info@schifferbooks.com
Web: www.schifferbooks.com

For our complete selection of fine books on this and related subjects, please visit our website at www.schifferbooks.com. You may also write for a free catalog.

Schiffer Publishing's titles are available at special discounts for bulk purchases for sales promotions or premiums. Special editions, including personalized covers, corporate imprints, and excerpts, can be created in large quantities for special needs. For more information, contact the publisher.

Bimba Landmann

ENCYCLOPEDIA

of My Imaginary Friends

Schiffer**Kids**®

4880 Lower Valley Road, Atglen, PA 19310

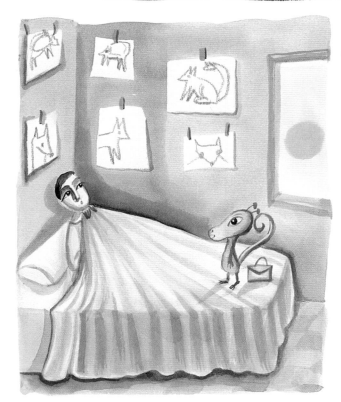

Table 1

Table 2

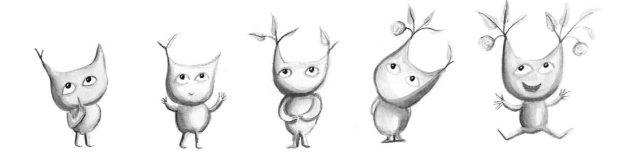

Plants

Humans

Table 3

1

2

3

4

5

6a

6b

6c

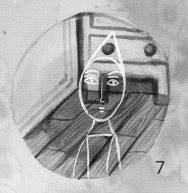

7

8

9

10

11

12

13

14

Animals

Table 4

Mythological and Fantastic Animals

1. Cosmic Snake
2. Kitsune
3. Phoenix
4. Griffin
5. Chimera
6. Pegasus
7. Firebird
8. Dragon
9. Unicorn

Table 5

The Incredibles *Table 6*

1. Spotty (spot on the wall)
2. Puddle
3. Cobbley (pebble on the table)
4. Crumby (bread crumb)
5. Big Piecey and Little Piecey (pieces of paper)
6. Mysterious (unidentified)
7. Twisted Mysterious
8. Little Rainbow Glass
9. Magic Ball (lucky charm)
10. $INXC ☼$ (blotch of paint)
11. Dusty (dust)
12. Tangle (bundle of yarn)
13. Invisible Manifold
14. ◉🗗∴↶≡⼃◻≡

The Realshaped *Table 7*

1. Shelter Blanket
2. Cloudy Pillow
3. Cup of Good Beginnings
4. Magic Pencil
5. Thousandtrips Shoe
6. Calming Pacifier
7. Doll Friend
8. Teddy Bear Friend
9. Soft Toy Friend
10. Shrieking Vacuum
11. Little Box
12. Scratch-Scratch Brush
13. Sweet Dreams Baby Bottle
14. Hairy Fork
15. Bold Spoon

Table 6

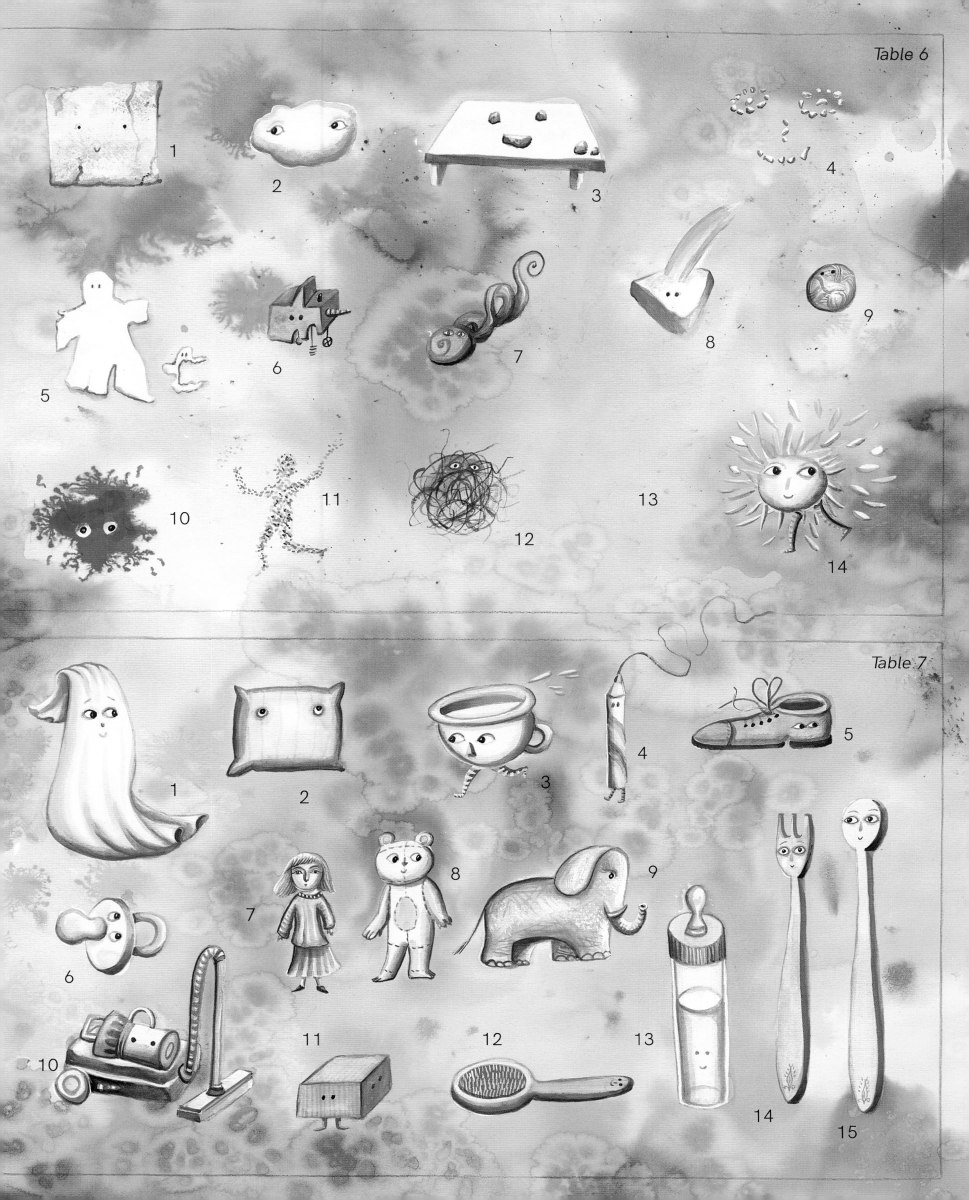

Table 7

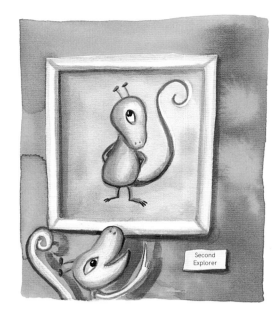

Second Explorer

First Explorer

Vegetable Companion

Museum

The Imaginationary

1. Friend of Pleasant Thoughts
2. Bouncy
3. Soft Flyer
4. The Evertogethers
5. Little One
6. Nameless
7. First Explorer
8. Second Explorer
9. Hairy
10. ⛾ᶰ≡ᴧ⛾
11. Moon Traveler
12. Spinny
13. Horsefish
14. Jumpy Fish
15. Magical Game Seeker
16. Sweetwhite
17. Night Companion
18. Multihair Man
19. Loyal Curly
20. Protector of Children
21. Halfmanhalfduck
22. Jump Mate
23. Silent
24. ⊡≡ᴧ∴Δ≡⊃⊂∼≡▣
25. Iggy Bump
26. Daring with Thorns
27. Daring with Fur
28. Third Explorer (its shape is still a secret)
29. Spiky Superplayful
30. Huggly Friend
31. The Without a Name (looking for one)
32. Little Master
33. Chaperone of Flights
34. Kind Giant
35. The Affectionate
36. Listener of Secrets
37. The Kind One
38. Appeaser of Dreams
39. Sweet Consoler
40. Problemsolver
41. Little Confidant
42. Colorful Ally
43. The Very-Old Great Master
(10,000,847,440,000,000 years old)

Table 8

Table 9

The Transformers

Cloud, the Queen of Transformations

She can transform into

1. Oval
2. Dog
3. Snake
4. Dragon
5. Elephant
6. Sheep
7. Unicorn
8. Fish
9. Bird
10. Child

. . . and countless other things.

Table 10

11. DragonChild
12. HorseFish
13. CrocoZebra
14. Playful (always changes its shape)
15. ChildTree
16. ViolinOwl
17. CatMouse
18. DolphHawk
19. DeerFlower

Table 11

The Naturals

The Imaginary Enemies (or Fake Friends)

1. Wisheater
2. Faultfinding Snake
3. Joystinger
4. Little Prankster
5. Pesky
6. Multieyes Humiliator
7. Courage Eater
8. The Insincere
9. The Serenity Twister
10. Patiencesmasher
11. Ideasdestroyer
12. Foul Play
13. Plan-Crushing Monster
14. The Stinging Ones
15. Confidence-Crushing Monster
16. The Unbearable
17. Enemy with the Antiempathy Stinger
18. The Dream Stomper
19. Antihope
20. FakeLove
21. The Deceiver
22. Fake Defender
23. Fake Friend Who Cares for Us
24. Bad Words
25. Hatemonger
26.
27. Manyheads of Constant Fighting
28. The Terrible (invisible)
29. The Monster of No-Respect
30. Stinging Words

Table 12

Table 13

Enemies

Speaking Animals

Mythological

Humans

Shadows

Incredibles

Mirrors

Realshapes

REALISTIC FORMS

Naturals

Plants

of Earth

Superheroes

Animals

Dinosaurs

of Fire

of Air

of Water

The Kingdom of Creativity

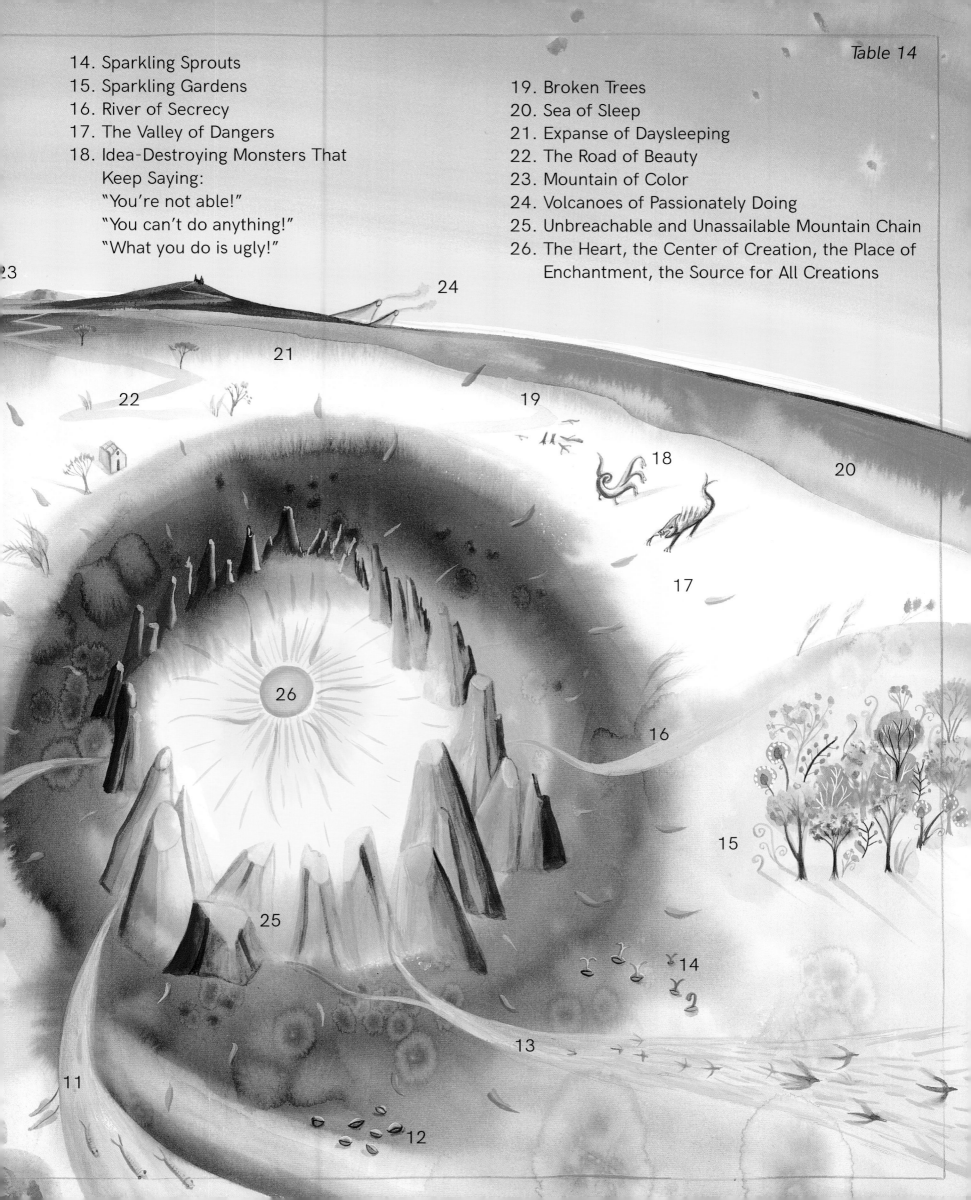

Table 14

14. Sparkling Sprouts
15. Sparkling Gardens
16. River of Secrecy
17. The Valley of Dangers
18. Idea-Destroying Monsters That
    Keep Saying:
    "You're not able!"
    "You can't do anything!"
    "What you do is ugly!"

19. Broken Trees
20. Sea of Sleep
21. Expanse of Daysleeping
22. The Road of Beauty
23. Mountain of Color
24. Volcanoes of Passionately Doing
25. Unbreachable and Unassailable Mountain Chain
26. The Heart, the Center of Creation, the Place of
    Enchantment, the Source for All Creations

Elements to Create

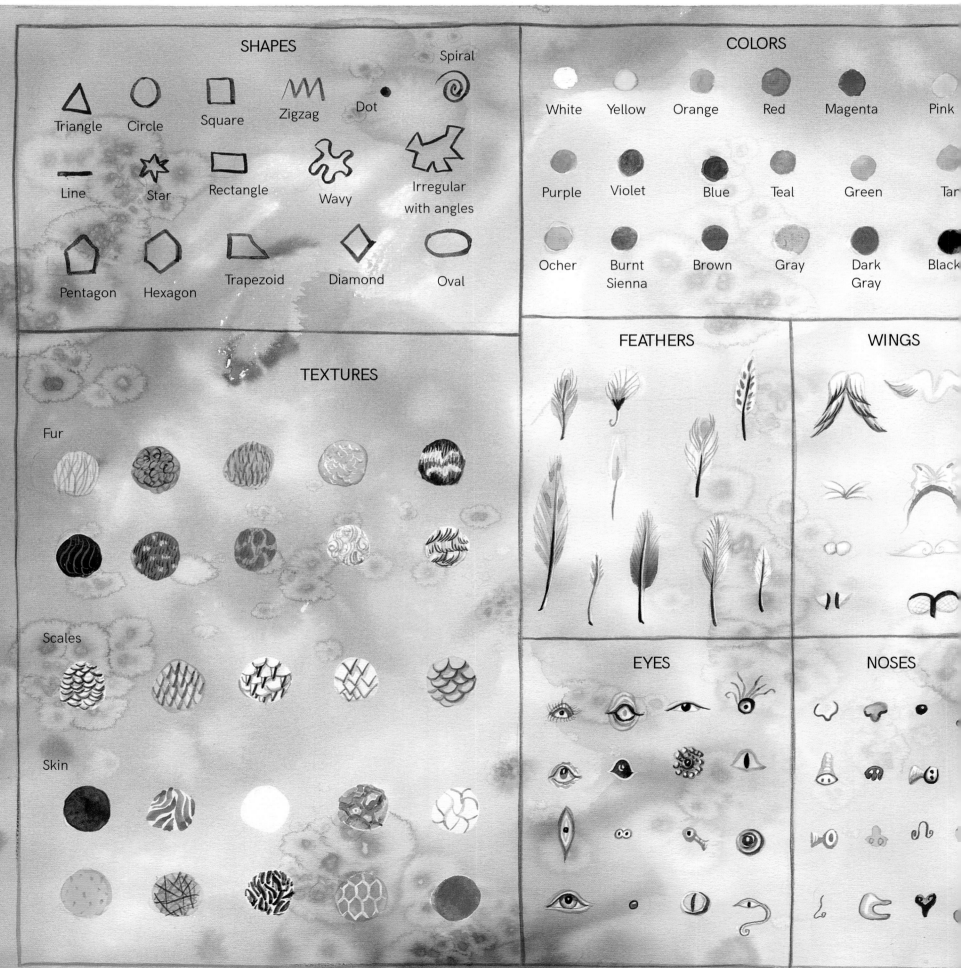

SHAPES

Triangle · Circle · Square · Zigzag · Dot · Spiral

Line · Star · Rectangle · Wavy · Irregular with angles

Pentagon · Hexagon · Trapezoid · Diamond · Oval

COLORS

White · Yellow · Orange · Red · Magenta · Pink

Purple · Violet · Blue · Teal · Green · Tan

Ocher · Burnt Sienna · Brown · Gray · Dark Gray · Black

TEXTURES

Fur

Scales

Skin

FEATHERS

WINGS

EYES

NOSES

an Imaginary Friend

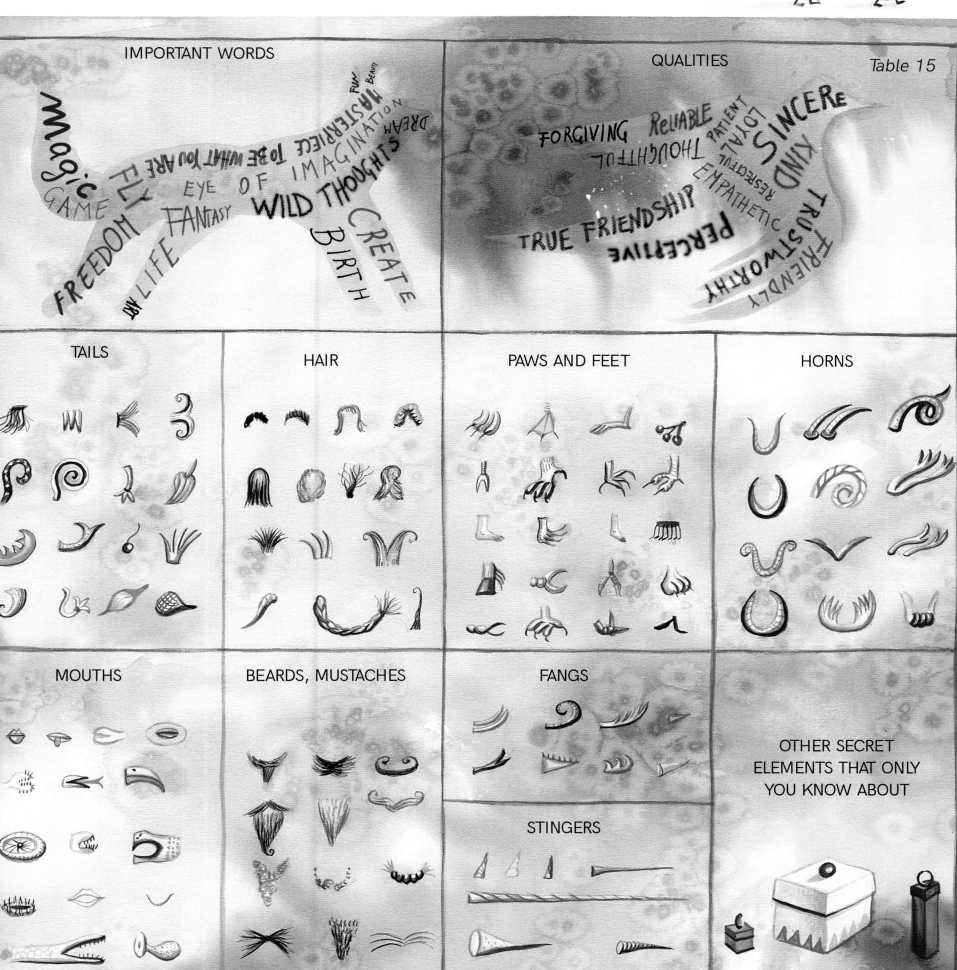

IMPORTANT WORDS

QUALITIES

Table 15

TAILS

HAIR

PAWS AND FEET

HORNS

MOUTHS

BEARDS, MUSTACHES

FANGS

STINGERS

OTHER SECRET
ELEMENTS THAT ONLY
YOU KNOW ABOUT

Creating

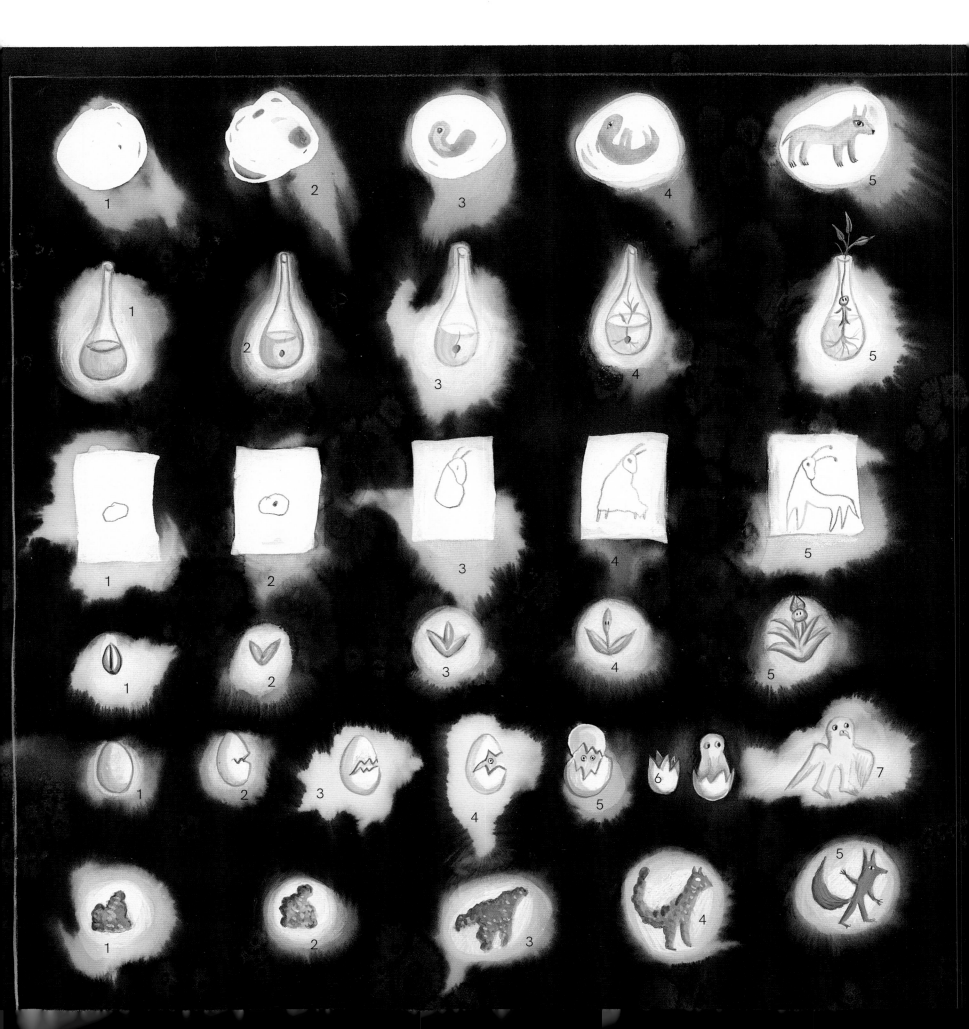

an Imaginary Friend

Table 16

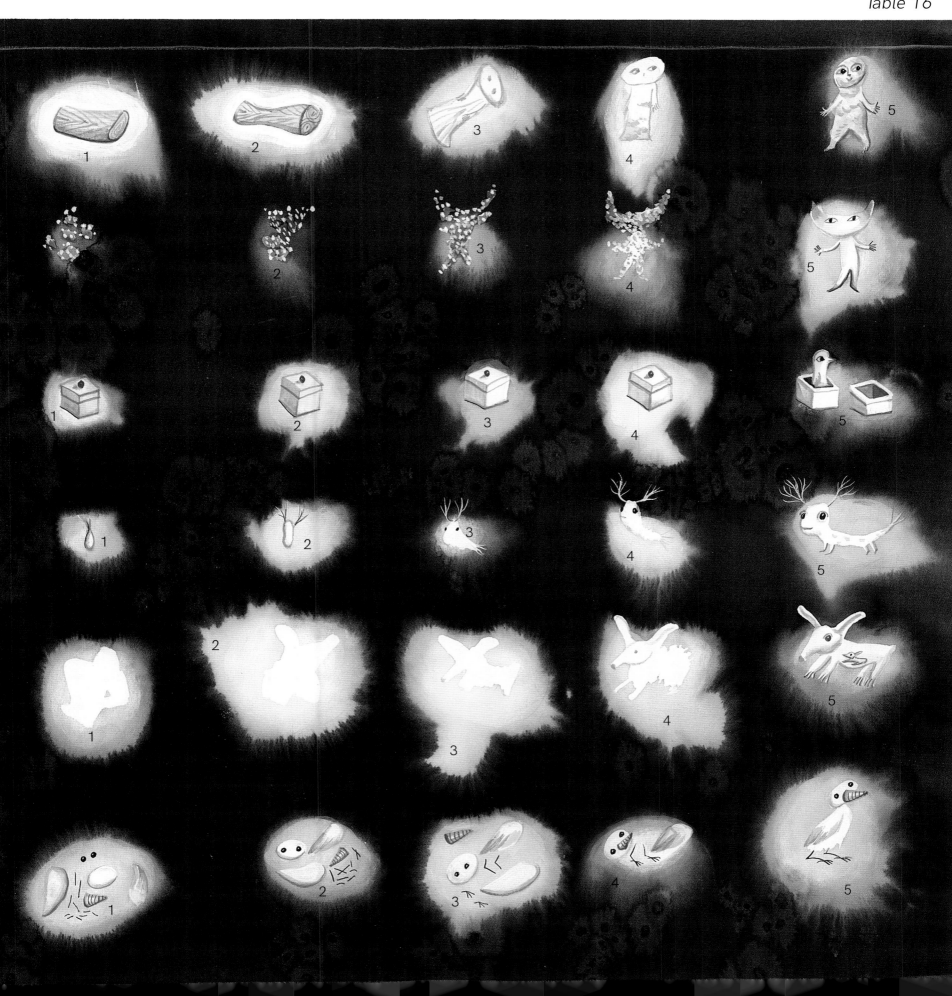

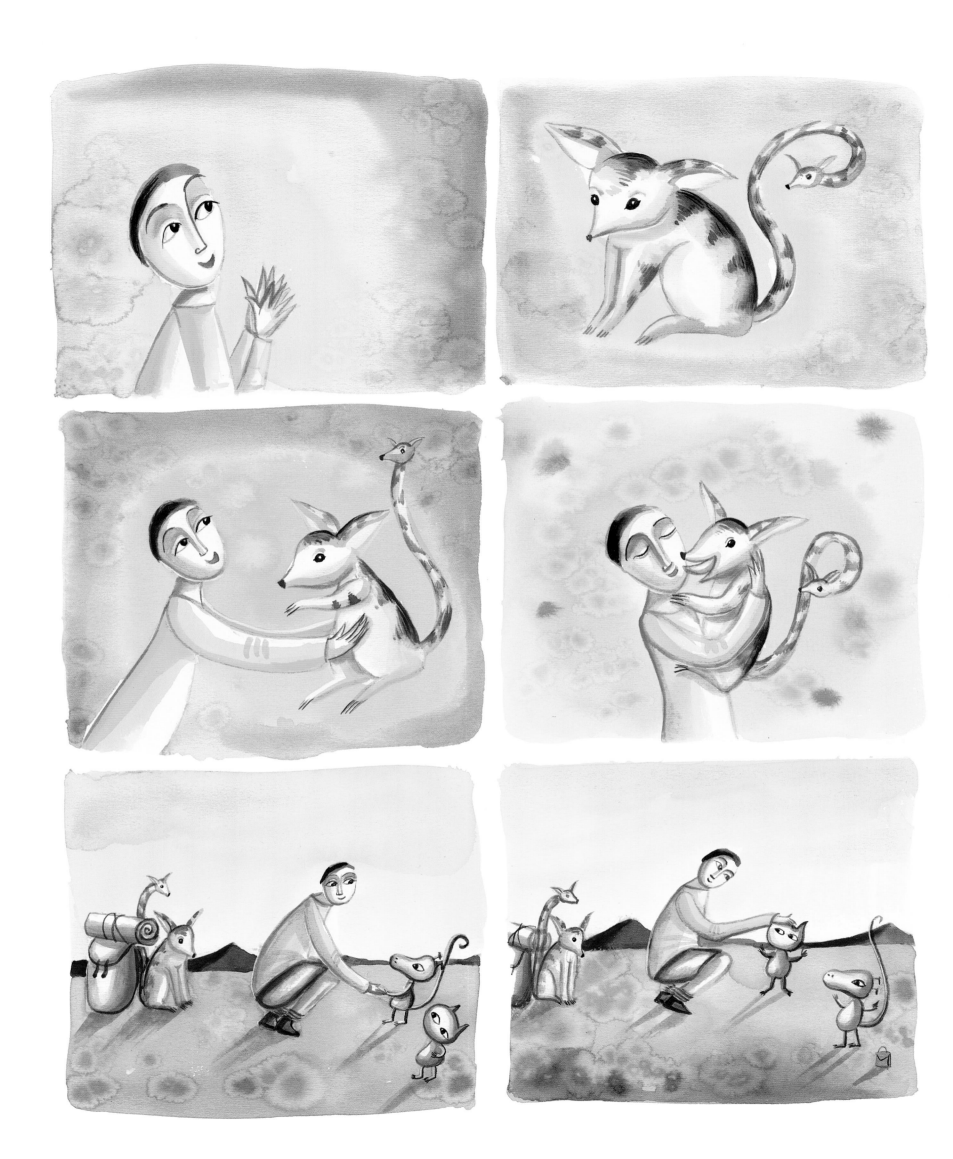

Creating a Home
Living Together

If the Imaginary Friend is small, it's easy to
1. build a home
2. bring it to visit its home
3. build it a bed in a matchbox
4. create a place for it to nap in a walnut
5. find a hidden place for it (sometimes, Imaginary Friends like to stay a secret)
6. give it a secret space
7. let it cool down in a small pool

If the Imaginary Friend is big or huge, it's more difficult to
8. bring it home
9. let it sleep in your bed
10. make it fit in the bathtub
11. find a food bowl for it
12. have a blanket that fits
13. fall asleep when it snores

Table 17

Table 18

1a

1b

1c

1d

2

3

4

5

6

7

8

9

10

Caring for the Creatures

1. Create a bond
2. Trust
3. First aid: taking care of them if they get hurt
4. Respect: respect their lifestyles, even if they are strange
5. Freedom: never tie them to things; never force them to do something
6. Kindness: take care of them in a loving way
7. For all their life
8. Education: teach them to behave and be independent
9. Playing
10. Cleaning, caring, wellness

Nourishment

Table 19

1

2

3

4

5

6

FOOD FOR THE BODY

1. Imaginary dinner, lunch, and breakfast
2. Imaginary water, drinks, and food
3. Imaginary treats (••• ⌘ ≋ ⌘ ⚛ ≡ △ ⌐ ⅲ and also ⟔⟡⟐ :))

FOOD FOR THE HEART

4. Feed fantasy and imagination by reading stories, admiring art, listening to music, and daydreaming
5. Enjoying the beauty of nature though meditation and contemplation
6. Feed creativity by making art with them, writing poems, acting, playing an instrument, drawing, painting, sculpting, making up stories, and creating things that don't exist

Anatomy

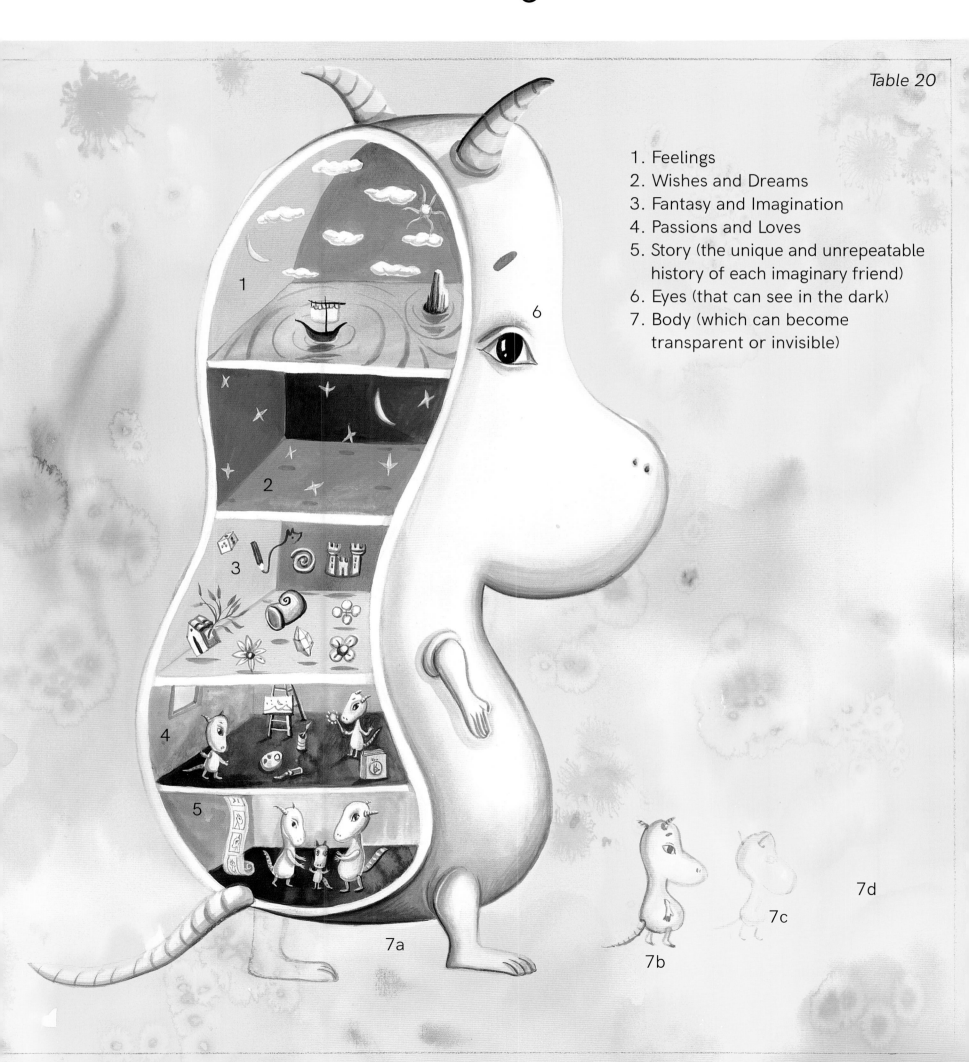

Table 20

1. Feelings
2. Wishes and Dreams
3. Fantasy and Imagination
4. Passions and Loves
5. Story (the unique and unrepeatable history of each imaginary friend)
6. Eyes (that can see in the dark)
7. Body (which can become transparent or invisible)

Table 21

Qualities
of an Imaginary Friend

1. Truthful: what it says and what it does are the same thing
2. Loyal and Faithful: connected to you by a true bond
3. Honest
4. Always available when you call it (you can call it by snapping your fingers, closing your eyes, saying its name, or however you wish)
5. Always on your side and by your side
6. Trustworthy: it'll never tell your secrets to anyone
7. Devoted: it'll never betray you
8. It'll never abandon you: you will be friends for your entire life!
9. Being magical, it can help you find things that have disappeared.
10. Sometimes, it makes your wishes come true.

1

2

3

BLA BLA BLA
BLA
BLA BLA
ZZT...

5

6

7

9

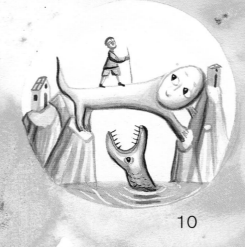

10

11

13

14

15

Table 22

Staying Together
Friendship

1. Playing
2. Running
3. Flying with imagination
4. Living incredible and impossible adventures
5. Practicing the art of conversation
6. Practicing the art of friendship
7. Practicing dealing with others (in discussions or when sharing ideas)
8. Telling secrets
9. Expressing fears and not feeling alone
10. Practicing how to overcome obstacles
11. Learning how to understand baffling things (even the completely mysterious ones of grown-ups)
12. Being listened to
13. Being comforted
14. Hugging
15. Challenging you to improve every day
16. Helping you to get to know yourself

The World Where Destinies Are Made

Table 23

1. Garden of Meetings
2. Hardworking City
3. Playground of Friendship
4. Horizon of Endless Traveling
5. Dreamy Peaks
6. Sea of Desires
7. Plain of Life
8. Path of Creativity
9. The Road of Art
10. Museum of Imaginary Friends
11. Tree of Life
12. Village of Tomorrow, the Future City Created by Children